SURVIVAL OF THE SALMON

Dear Riley,

Something fishy is going on in the North Atlantic Ocean, causing the wild salmon there to become endangered!

Join me, Aunt Martha and Cousin Alice in Alaska for the yearly Pacific salmon migration. Since wild Pacific salmon are doing well, studying them may give us ideas that can help their North Atlantic relatives. We'll count fish on foot, from counting towers and even from a plane.

Be sure to bring your waders!

"Catch" you later!

Uncle Max

ADVENTURES OF RILEY

BY AMANDA LUMRY & LAURA HURWITZ

Eaglemont Press

All photographs by Amanda Lumry except:
cover grizzly bear © Daisy Gilardini/Alaska Stock
cover sockeye salmon © Mark Emery/Alaska Stock
pg. 12 sockeye/red salmon © John Warden/Alaska Stock
pg. 13 eagle © Tom Mangelsen/Images of Nature
pg. 14 moose © Calvin W. Hall/Alaska Stock
pg. 27 two grizzly bears © Eric Baccega/Nature Picture Library

Illustrations and Layouts by Ulkutay & Ulkutay, London WC2E 9RZ
Editing and Digital Compositing by Michael E. Penman

Digital Imaging by Embassy Graphics, Canada
Printed in China by Phoenix Asia
ISBN-10: 0-9748411-3-7
ISBN-13: 978-0-9748411-3-7

A special thanks to all the scientists who collaborated on this project. Your time and assistance are very much appreciated.

A portion of the proceeds from your purchase of this licensed product supports the stated educational mission of the Smithsonian Institution - "the increase and diffusion of knowledge." The name of the Smithsonian Institution and the sunburst logo are registered trademarks of the Smithsonian Institution and are registered in the U.S. Patent and Trademark Office.
www.si.edu

2% of the proceeds from this book will be donated to the Wildlife Conservation Society.
http://wcs.org

A royalty of approximately 1% of the estimated retail price of this book will be received by World Wildlife Fund (WWF). The Panda Device and WWF are registered trademarks. All rights reserved by World Wildlife Fund, Inc.
www.worldwildlife.org

574.5

First edition published 2006 by
Eaglemont Press
PMB 741
15600 NE 8th #B-1
Bellevue, WA 98008
1-877-590-9744
info@eaglemontpress.com
www.eaglemontpress.com

Library of Congress Cataloging-in-Publication Data

Lumry, Amanda.
   Survival of the salmon / by Amanda Lumry & Laura Hurwitz.
      p. cm. – (Adventures of Riley)
   Summary: Riley and Alice visit the wilderness of southeastern Alaska to help discover why Pacific Salmon are thriving while North Atlantic Salmon are more endangered than ever, and meet a variety of animals and a well-known animal expert along the way.
   ISBN-13: 978-0-9748411-3-7 (hardcover : alk. paper)
   ISBN-10: 0-9748411-3-7 (hardcover : alk. paper)
   [1. Salmon–Fiction. 2. Zoology–Alaska–Fiction. 3. Alaska–Fiction.] I. Hurwitz, Laura. II. Title.
   PZ7.L9787155Sur 2006
   [Fic]–dc22
                              2005026196

"Why can't I just share my room with Sophie?" asked Riley.

"I thought you'd be excited to move to a new room," his mother said.

"I'm used to this one, just like I was used to third grade. Why does everything have to change when you grow up?" His mother smiled.

"We'll talk about it when you get back from Alaska," she said.

3

When Riley landed in Southeast Alaska, everyone ran to greet him.

"I can't wait to get started," Riley said, "but why is everybody wearing bells?"

"To keep the bears away, silly," said Alice.

"What bears? I thought we were tracking salmon," said Riley.

"We are," said Uncle Max. "Salmon have an important job. After living two to three years in the ocean, they must return to their birthplace to lay their eggs, or *spawn*. But predators, usually bears, catch them before they can get to their final destination."

Sea Lion

➤ A male sea lion (2,400lbs, 1,100kg) is three times larger than a female (770lbs, 350kg).

➤ A sea lion can dive to 1,300ft (400m) deep.

➤ The killer whale (orca) is the sea lion's main predator.

Bruce W. Robson, Marine Wildlife and Fisheries Biologist, World Wildlife Fund

Orca

➤ In medieval times, the word *orca* meant *sea-monster*.

➤ It is the world's largest predator of mammals.

➤ Sailors used to call the orca a "whale killer" because they saw orcas attack larger whales. This name was later changed to "killer whale."

James Mead, Division of Mammals, National Museum of Natural History, Smithsonian Institution

The Nikole
ALASKA

Leaving the airport, th drove past the harbor on the way to the float plane ramp

Sea Otter

➤ A sea otter's fur has up to one million hairs per square inch (150,000 per square cm).
➤ It uses rocks to crack open the shellfish it eats.
➤ It is the smallest marine mammal.

Margaret Williams, Director, Bering Sea Program, World Wildlife Fund

"We will need to fly to camp," said Aunt Martha. "There aren't many roads here, so most people use boats or planes to get around."

Using the ocean as a runway, they took off, flying over many rivers and glaciers on their way to camp.

Glacier

➤ Currently, 10% of the land worldwide is covered by glaciers.

➤ 75% of the earth's fresh water is stored in glaciers.

➤ A glacier can be retreating (shrinking) or advancing (growing).

➤ When ice breaks off of a glacier, the act is called "calving."

Maxwell "Uncle Max" Plimpton, Professor and Senior Field Biologist

They landed on a wide spot in the river and set up camp. That night, the woods came alive with the HOOTS and HOWLS of unseen nightlife. Riley glanced around nervously.

"It's okay," said Uncle Max. "Those animals sound close, but they're not. To keep them from getting close, we let them know we're here by clanging bear bells, talking loudly and singing."

"Singing?" asked Riley. "What do I sing?"

"Anything that pops into your head," said Aunt Martha. "The louder, the better."

Sockeye Salmon

➤ A sockeye salmon turns from silver to bright red as it migrates from the ocean to spawn in freshwater rivers and lakes.

➤ Once a sockeye leaves the ocean to spawn, it stops eating.

➤ Sockeye salmon use their sense of smell during migration to sniff out and find the exact stream (or lake) they were hatched in.

Steve Zack, PhD, Pacific West Coordinator, Wildlife Conservation Society

In the morning, Aunt Martha flew low and slow over the river to spot groups of salmon and radio their position to Uncle Max.

"Why are we counting the salmon, Uncle Max?" asked Riley.

"To see if the salmon population is growing or declining. Fish are monitored carefully in Alaska, so there will be a healthy supply year after year. In the North Atlantic Ocean, though, commercial over-fishing, pollution and dams create big problems for the wild salmon. These dangers make it harder for the North Atlantic salmon to spawn."

"What do salmon do the rest of the year?" asked Riley.

1. Male and female salmon spawn in freshwater streams. Females produce thousands of eggs and males fertilize them. Fertilized eggs are put in a redd.

"They have very busy and short lives," answered Uncle Max.

4.

Most salmon will die naturally after spawning, while some are eaten by predators. Their bodies will then break down and enrich the stream, creating a healthy environment in which the new eggs will hatch.

Then the cycle begins all over again!

2.

The baby fish, or fry, grow in fresh water, such as a stream or lake, for up to two years. After that, they migrate to the ocean.

These migrating salmon, called smolts, undergo changes that will allow them to live in salt water.

3.

Smolts feed and grow in the ocean until they become adult salmon. Up to four years after hatching, adult salmon will return to their birth stream to spawn.

Uncle Max pointed out a redd, an area on the river bottom where a female salmon used her tail to brush gravel over her eggs to protect them.

"I count about two hundred salmon so far," he said, collecting a water sample. "Can you mark that down for me, Alice...Alice?"

Bald Eagle

➤ The bald eagle is really not bald. The word *balde* means "white" in Old English.

➤ The male and female bald eagle look alike, but the female is 25% larger.

➤ The bald eagle may have the largest nest of any bird. It can take three months to build.

Carla Dove, Ph.D., Research Scientist (Ornithologist), National Museum of Natural History, Smithsonian Institution

Alice and Riley had wandered off on their own. "Salmon are so boring," Alice sighed.

"Not that one," said Riley, pointing to a lively fish leaping its way upriver.

SWOOOSH! A giant bald eagle swooped down and snatched the jumping salmon.

"Did you see that?" asked Riley.

"Of course. Now come on, my dad's already at the fish counting tower," snapped Alice.

13

"Since when did your dad grow antlers?" asked Riley. Uncle Max stood on top of the tower, waving wildly. On the ground below him was...A GIANT MOOSE!

"Don't look him in the eye or he might charge," said Riley. Thinking quickly, they jumped behind a nearby rock and hid until the moose snorted and stomped off.

Moose

➤ The moose is the largest member of the deer family.

➤ Newborn calves weigh 28-35lbs (13-16kg), and within five months, grow to over 300lbs (136kg).

➤ A female moose with calves has been known to charge at people, cars or even trains!

Don E. Wilson,
Senior Scientist,
Smithsonian
Institution

15

"That was close!" said Uncle Max.

"So was the mean bald eagle that attacked the salmon we were watching," said Riley.

"Eagles aren't mean, just hungry. When the salmon are running, the river is like a fast food restaurant for predators," said Uncle Max.

"Now I know why the salmon are running!" laughed Alice.

After some
fast food of their
own, Aunt Martha flew
Riley and Alice along the river.

17

The salmon's red scales sparkled in the sunlight.

"I want to get a picture of this," said Alice.

"Riley, could you keep your head down?"

"No problem," he groaned.

"Gross!" said Alice. "Mom, Riley's turning green."

"Maybe we'd better get back on solid ground," said Aunt Martha.

Riley looked out the window. "Why aren't there any fish in that stream down there?" he asked.

"Let's fly over it again and see," Aunt Martha said. Riley moaned and grabbed the airsick bag. "On second thought, maybe you should check it out on foot tomorrow."

19

That night, Riley imagined that he was a salmon, facing all sorts of dangers on his way back home.

At sunrise, they hiked to the stream they had seen from the plane. The salmon count here was much lower than Uncle Max expected.

SPLATT!

"The mosquitoes are everywhere!" Alice complained.

HOO! HOO!

AWOOOOOO... AWOOOOOO...

"What's that?" asked Alice.

Gray Wolf

➤ A gray wolf doesn't have to be gray. Multiple pups from the same litter may be white, brown, gray or black.

➤ There are 6,000-9,000 wild wolves living in Alaska.

➤ A wolf can go for days, or even weeks, without food, but when it eats, it can eat as much as 22lbs (10kg) of meat at once.

Denise Woods, Research Assistant, WWF Bering Sea Ecoregion Program, World Wildlife Fund

"Two good reasons to keep up with your dad!" said Riley. Alice's bear bells jingled loudly as they hurried to catch up with Uncle Max.

Great Horned Owl

➤ It gets its name from the large, horn-like ear tufts on its head.

➤ It is one of the largest American owls, growing as tall as 23½in (60cm).

➤ It is mostly active at night, using its excellent night vision and sense of hearing to hunt prey.

Claudia Angle, Museum Specialist, USGS Birds, National Museum of Natural History, Smithsonian Institution

23

"Alice, why don't you show Riley the new fish finder?" asked Uncle Max.

"Cool!" said Alice. "You stick this end in the water and..."

WHOOSH! Two seagulls dove in between them.

The fish finder flew up into the air and crashed onto the rocks.

"Alice, are you okay?" asked Uncle Max.

"I'm fine, but I think the screen is cracked," said Alice.

"Don't worry," said Riley. "I bet we can connect the fish finder to my video game player! They both use the same kind of cord." Riley plugged the units together while Uncle Max placed the fish finder's sonar into the stream.

"Hey, I think it's working. I see two blips on the video game screen!" said Uncle Max. "Carrot Top, you're a genius!" Riley blushed.

"Um, Dad," Alice whispered nervously. "I think I know why there aren't many salmon in this stream."

"Why?" asked Uncle Max.

"The bears are eating them," said Alice.

"Of course bears are eating salmon, Alice. That's nothing new," said Uncle Max.

"I mean THOSE bears!" Alice hissed.

"What do we do?" Riley's heart was pounding. *Climb a tree? Sing? Run?*

Grizzly Bear

➤ A grizzly bear is actually a type of brown bear, getting its name from its "grizzled" looking fur.

➤ It can weigh up to 2,200lbs (998kg)–that's over one ton!

➤ It will hibernate for up to six months during the winter when food is scarce.

Jack Hanna, Director Emeritus, Columbus Zoo; Host, "Into the Wild" TV series

"*Back away, back away,*" sang a voice behind them. One step...two steps...three steps. Moving very slowly, they finally reached safety. They turned to thank the mysterious stranger who helped them.

"Jungle Jack!" exclaimed Riley.

"You know Mr. Hanna?" asked Alice.

"I watch his show every week!" said Riley.

"Well, if it isn't Professor Maxwell Plimpton and little Alice," said Jack. "I haven't seen you in ages."

"This is my nephew, Riley," Uncle Max said.

At camp, Aunt Martha made them all big mugs of hot chocolate.

"What brings you all to Alaska?" asked Jack.

"The salmon migration," Riley told him.

"I'm studying grizzly bears," said Jack. "I guess you'd say my research is eating your research. But that's the way nature works. Most of these salmon have spawned and will die soon anyway."

30

"I get it!" said Riley. "Then the baby salmon swim back to the ocean and the migration cycle will start all over again."

"Right! Plus, the bears need to chow down to store up fat for hibernation." Jack took one last sip. "That hit the spot! I'd better get back to work. It's a big planet, but I'm sure we will run into each other again."

"Between hungry bears and Jungle Jack, salmon just got a lot more interesting," said Alice.

"I think salmon are cool," said Riley. "Even though they face difficult situations, they keep going and going. They never give up!"

"That's right, Riley," said Uncle Max. "As tough as the migration may seem, the strongest and luckiest Pacific salmon do survive. I hope to find a way to give wild North Atlantic salmon the same chance!"

"If only they could call a place like this home," Aunt Martha said, hugging everyone. "A clean, safe place where the only dangers are natural ones."

North Atlantic Salmon

➤ Wild North Atlantic salmon can be found on both sides of the Atlantic Ocean.

➤ The species is in danger due to human activity such as pollution, dams and over-fishing.

➤ 85 times more farmed Atlantic salmon are caught than wild North Atlantic salmon.

Bruce Collette, Senior Systematic Zoologist, National Marine Fisheries Service, Smithsonian Institution

33

Back home, Riley told everyone about the salmon, the moose, the bald eagle, the bears and, of course, Jack Hanna. He realized that as you grow, things change, and having a new room wasn't so bad after all.

He returned to living the life of a nine-year old, until he received another letter from his Uncle Max.

Where will Riley go next?

FURTHER INFORMATION

Glossary:

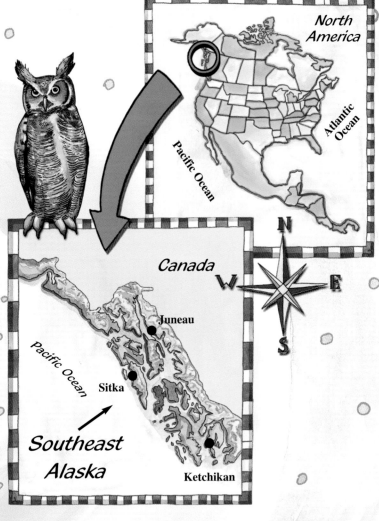

ENRICH: To make better or stronger.

FERTILIZE: To add something so it will grow.

FISH COUNTING TOWER: A high platform built along the bank of a stream or river, allowing the viewer to see and count fish as they swim by.

FISH FINDER: A tool that uses sonar (sound waves) to locate fish under water. A screen shows digital images of the fish.

FLOAT PLANE: A plane on top of floating pontoons, instead of wheels, so it can take off and land on water.

MIGRATE: To travel from one place to another, often because of changing climate and/or moving food sources.

FRY: A small, recently hatched fish.

PREDATOR: An animal who hunts and eats other animals.

REDD: A "nest" made by salmon, where they lay their eggs on the floors of riverbeds.

SMOLT: Young adult salmon. These fish travel from fresh water rivers to the ocean.

SPAWN: To lay many eggs.

We are thrilled that Jack Hanna could join Riley on this Alaskan adventure! "Jungle Jack" is known to millions as one of the world's most beloved and respected naturalists. He visits cities all across the United States to talk about his amazing animal and travel experiences. Plus, he is the host of the popular television series *Jack Hanna's Into the Wild*.

As Director Emeritus of the Columbus Zoo, he transformed this once outdated, enclosed cage style facility into one of the best natural habitat parks in the United States. His love of animals began in his childhood on his father's farm outside Knoxville, Tennessee. Jack considers wildlife conservation his true calling and encourages others to follow in his footsteps. In addition to his speaking engagements, he is also a regular guest on such television shows as *Larry King Live*, *Good Morning America* and the *Late Show with David Letterman*.

WHAT IS THIS?

➤ Hidden inside each *Adventures of Riley* book is at least one compass.

➤ Each one will unlock an on-line Further Adventure movie on Riley's website.

Visit Riley's World today!

www.adventuresofriley.com